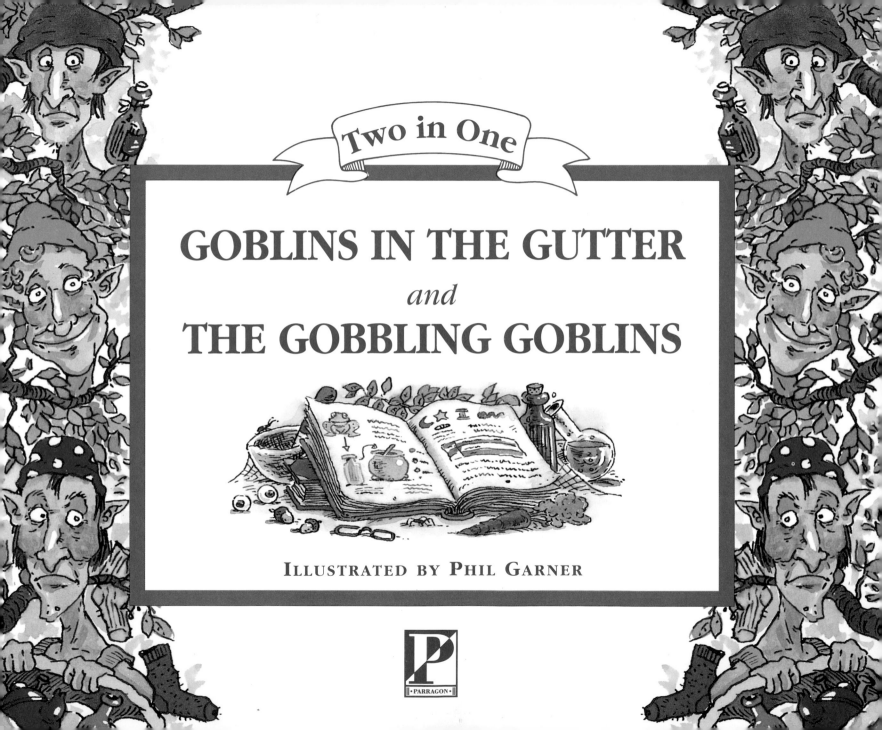

Two in One

GOBLINS IN THE GUTTER

and

THE GOBBLING GOBLINS

ILLUSTRATED BY PHIL GARNER

P
· PARRAGON ·

This is a Parragon Book

©Parragon 1997

Parragon
13-17 Avonbridge Trading Estate
Atlantic Road, Avonmouth
Bristol. BS11 9QD

Produced by The Templar Company plc,
Pippbrook Mill, London Road, Dorking,
Surrey RH4 1JE

Designed by Janie Louise Hunt
Edited by Caroline Steeden
Printed and bound in Italy
ISBN 0 75252 502 6

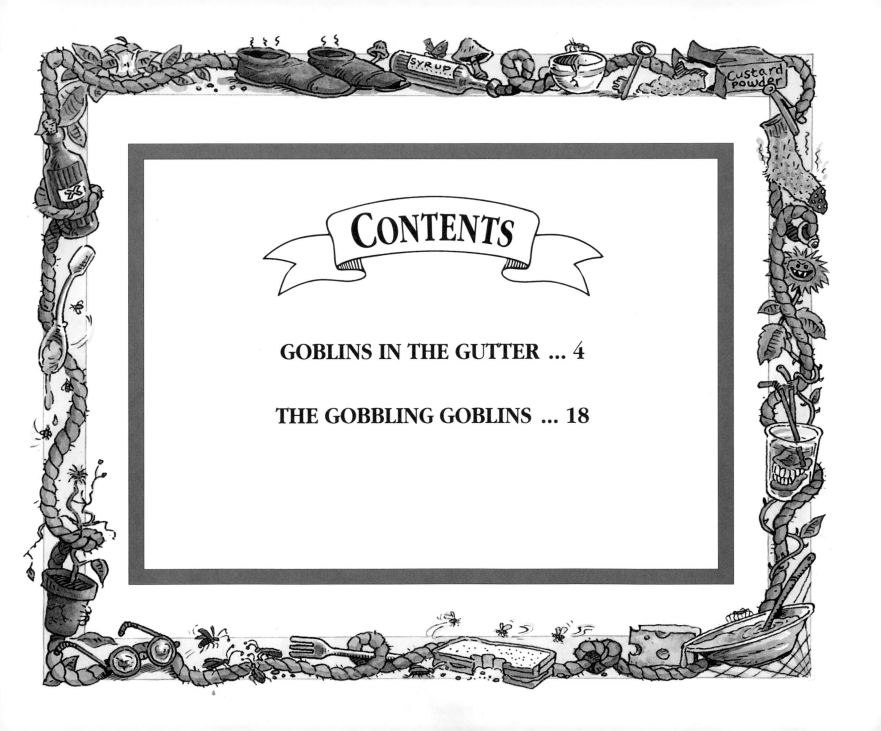

CONTENTS

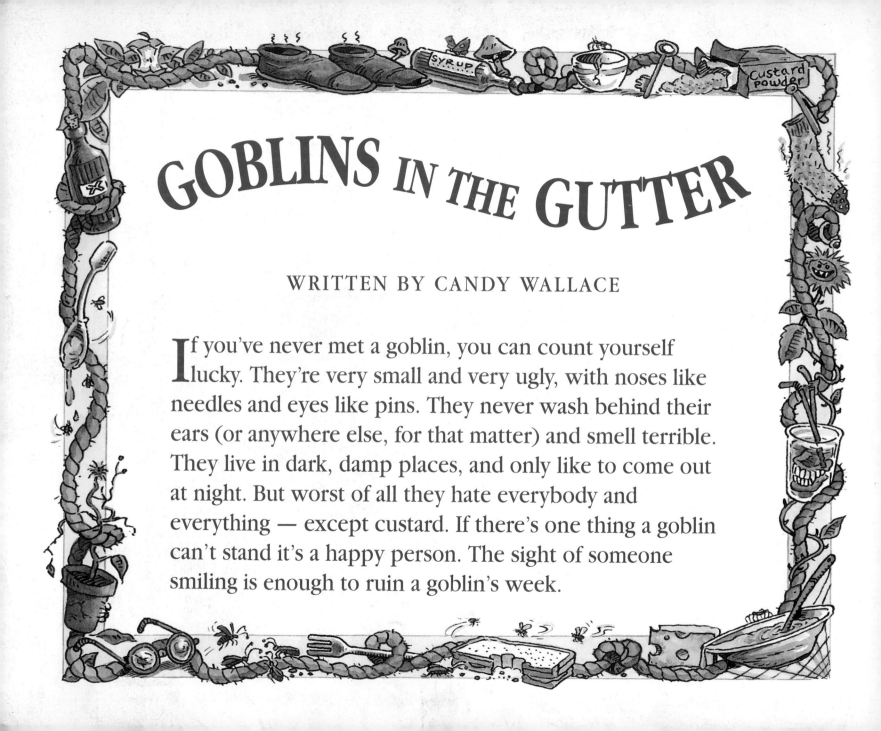

GOBLINS IN THE GUTTER

WRITTEN BY CANDY WALLACE

If you've never met a goblin, you can count yourself lucky. They're very small and very ugly, with noses like needles and eyes like pins. They never wash behind their ears (or anywhere else, for that matter) and smell terrible. They live in dark, damp places, and only like to come out at night. But worst of all they hate everybody and everything — except custard. If there's one thing a goblin can't stand it's a happy person. The sight of someone smiling is enough to ruin a goblin's week.

There was once a little girl called Poppy who was always happy. She had a nice mum and dad and an older brother called Fred. Now if you've got an older brother, you probably think he's a pain in the neck. But Poppy thought Fred was the best thing since beefburgers.

"I'm really lucky to have a brother like him," she would say to her friends.

Poppy thought school was absolutely brilliant, too. There was nothing she liked more than two pages of sums to do — unless it was three pages of sums. Everybody else thought Miss Crochet the teacher was horrible and grumpy and made them work too hard. They put chewing gum on her chair and daddy-long-legs in her desk to make her screech. But Poppy thought she was funny and laughed at her.

Outside Poppy's house in Acacia Avenue there was a drain in the road. If you looked down it all you could see was dirty water at the bottom. It was dark and smelly and full of old lolly sticks, dead leaves and spiders. There were goblins living in that drain. You couldn't see them, but if you knelt down and put your ear to the ground you might have heard them arguing. Goblins are always arguing and fighting.

They had moved there when Chestnut Tree Close was dug up to lay new water pipes. They hadn't minded the noisy road drills. But laughing workmen who sang loud songs and told jokes were more than a goblin could stomach. So, at dead of night, they had packed up and made their way to Acacia Avenue, and the drain outside Poppy's house.

They soon realised this was a big mistake.

"It makes me feel sick," said Gruel, the oldest, grumpiest goblin, "every time I see Whatshername skipping along to school with a big smile on her face. She should be arrested for humming without due care and attention."

"Well I think we should sort her out," said a fat goblin called Squelch, who thought all children should be made into savoury pies. "If we can't wipe that smile off her face, I'm a pixie."

The next morning, two goblins popped their heads through the grille of the drain. Their mean little eyes darted about to make sure no one was around. They jumped out holding a length of dirty old string, tied one end to the drain and tiptoed across the pavement to tie the other end to the hedge outside Poppy's house.

"There's nothing like a couple of grazed knees to make children cry!" sniggered one. "Let's hope she enjoys the trip!" giggled the other and they jumped back inside the drain to wait and listen.

Sure enough, a few minutes later there was a cry and a commotion. Gleefully the goblins peeped out to survey their handiwork. But it wasn't Poppy they saw on the pavement — it was an old man, sitting with arms and legs waving in the air!

"Oh dear, oh dear!" said the old man. "Whatever happened? Thank goodness nothing's broken. That could have been a nasty fall!"

Poppy's mum and dad rushed out of the house to help him. So did Mr Entwhistle from across the road and Mrs Ramsbottom from number 67 .

"Are you all right, dear?" asked Poppy's mum, who was very worried about the old man. "Come on in and have a nice cup of tea. What horrid children would tie string across the path like that! Just wait till I catch them!"

"When you've had a nice cuppa I'll take you home," said Mrs Ramsbottom, anxiously.

"Thank you so much!" replied the old man, as they helped him out of the hedge. "Do you know, I've lived in this street for two years and no one has ever spoken to me before!" They all went into Poppy's house. "Well you can come round for tea any time, Mr — er —."

"Brown. Ernest Brown," said the old man, and smiled to himself happily.

"Rats!" hissed Spodworthy, Goblin-in-Chief, to Gruel. "We got the wrong person! We'd better get it right next time! All we've done is make someone else happy too!"

That night, Squelch crept along the drains underground up the pipes and through the plughole into the kitchen sink in Poppy's house. There on the table was her lunchbox for school, which Poppy's mum always packed the night before. He scurried to the rubbish bin and picked out a horrible smelly half-eaten fish. Then he opened her lunch box, took out all the cheese from the sandwiches and put the fish in instead! He threw the cheese in the bin, and put Poppy's chocolate cake in his pocket for later!

"If that doesn't make her cry at school today, I don't know what will!" he smirked, and dived back down the plughole. Squelch couldn't think of anything worse than going without your lunch...

Poppy was none the wiser. In the morning she walked out of the garden gate holding her lunchbox and humming a tune. Before long, she noticed a little cat following her, jumping up at the lunchbox and swiping it with her paw.

"Hello pussycat!" said Poppy, bending down to stroke her. "Oh dear, you look very thin and your fur is all matted and dull. Haven't you got a home?"

The little cat gave a feeble miaow and sniffed and pawed at her lunch box.

"You can have a sandwich if you like," said Poppy, and opened up her box. When she saw the fish sandwiches, she laughed. "Poor Mum must have been a bit muddled last night!" she said. "Come on, pussycat. Fred's always wanted a cat and you need someone to look after you."

Poppy picked up the cat and took her home. Fred was thrilled.

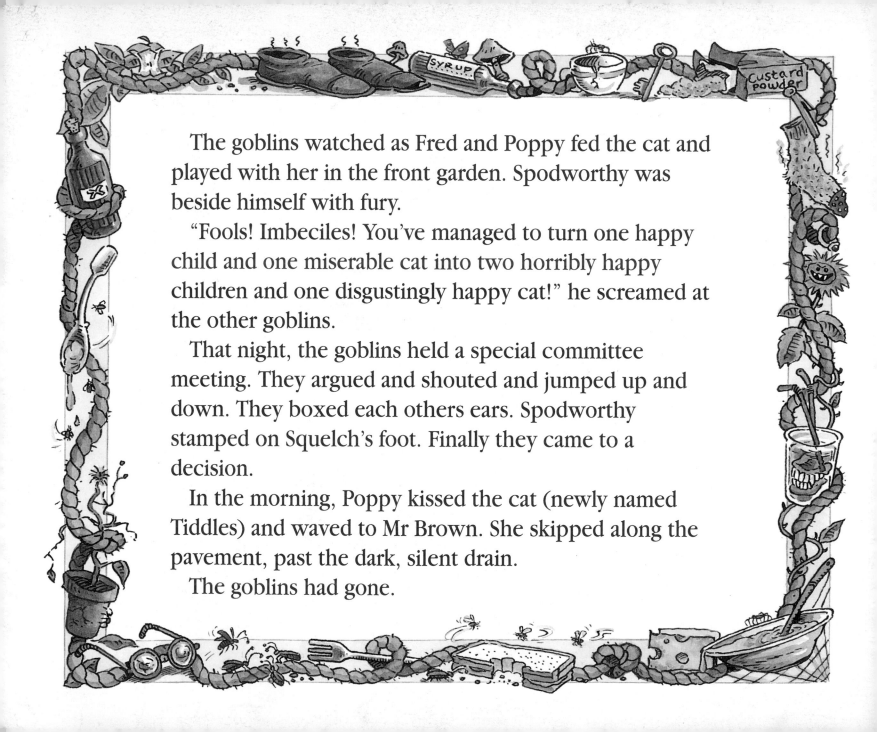

The goblins watched as Fred and Poppy fed the cat and played with her in the front garden. Spodworthy was beside himself with fury.

"Fools! Imbeciles! You've managed to turn one happy child and one miserable cat into two horribly happy children and one disgustingly happy cat!" he screamed at the other goblins.

That night, the goblins held a special committee meeting. They argued and shouted and jumped up and down. They boxed each others ears. Spodworthy stamped on Squelch's foot. Finally they came to a decision.

In the morning, Poppy kissed the cat (newly named Tiddles) and waved to Mr Brown. She skipped along the pavement, past the dark, silent drain.

The goblins had gone.

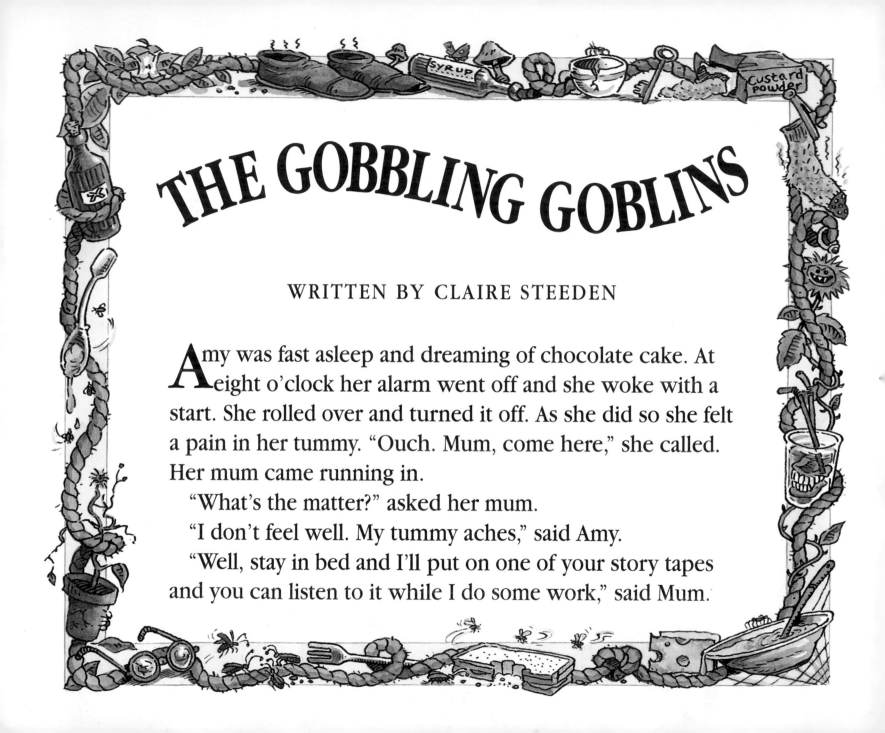

THE GOBBLING GOBLINS

WRITTEN BY CLAIRE STEEDEN

Amy was fast asleep and dreaming of chocolate cake. At eight o'clock her alarm went off and she woke with a start. She rolled over and turned it off. As she did so she felt a pain in her tummy. "Ouch. Mum, come here," she called. Her mum came running in.

"What's the matter?" asked her mum.

"I don't feel well. My tummy aches," said Amy.

"Well, stay in bed and I'll put on one of your story tapes and you can listen to it while I do some work," said Mum.

Amy snuggled into her duvet listening to a story about goblins, and gazing at the doll's house in the corner of her room. After a while she felt sleepy, but as she began to doze she thought she saw two little faces looking out through her doll's house window. She woke again later, when her mum came into the room. "How are you feeling?" asked Mum.

"I still feel a bit poorly. I just had a funny dream about goblins living in my doll's house," said Amy.

"There aren't any goblins in your doll's house, silly," laughed Mum.

"I wish there were. It would be fun," said Amy.

"No it wouldn't. Goblins are usually very naughty," said Mum. "Are you hungry? Would you like some lunch?"

"Not really," mumbled Amy.

"Well, how about a nice boiled egg with soldiers?" suggested Mum.

Amy followed her mum downstairs and lay on the sofa watching television while mum made lunch.

"Eat up," said Mum, as she set down a tray in front of Amy.

"But I don't feel very hungry," whined Amy.

"How about if I help you?" asked Mum, and she dipped the spoon into the egg. "O.K.," smiled Amy.

Just as the spoon got close to Amy's mouth, the phone rang and her Mum turned away to answer it. Amy was about to eat the egg when two goblins ran out from behind the salt and pepper pots, jumped up and ate all the egg off the spoon. Amy could not believe her eyes! They looked just like the goblins in her dream. They ran back to their hiding place, giggling.

Amy's Mum put the phone down, turned back to Amy and looked at the spoon.

"So you are hungry after all," said Mum.

"I didn't eat it. It was the goblins hiding behind the pepper pot," said Amy, pointing to the tray. "Didn't you see them?"

"No," said Mum. "You and your goblins. Let's get on with lunch."

"But I'm not hungry," said Amy.

"Well, you soon gobbled the last spoonful. I know, if I look away maybe the goblins will eat it again," laughed Mum. She was happy to play Amy's game if it meant she ate her lunch. So she dipped a soldier into the egg, held it in front of Amy, and looked away.

Amy sat and stared in amazement as again the goblins dashed out, ate the food and ran back.

Amy started to giggle because they looked so funny. Mum turned back and saw that the soldier had gone.

"Who could have eaten that?" asked Mum with a smile.

"The goblins ate it," laughed Amy.

"They must be hungry. Let's give them some more," said mum. Amy and her mum sat on the sofa playing this game while the goblins ran back and forth eating Amy's lunch, until it was all gone. "That was fun," said Amy.

"Good," said Mum. "Lie here and watch television, and you'll soon start to feel better now you've eaten." As Mum left the room the goblins crept out and called to Amy. "Psstt, thanks for lunch."

"That's all right. I wasn't hungry. Where did you come from?" asked Amy.

"Oh, we live in a lovely little house upstairs," replied the goblins.

"What! In my doll's house? So it *was* your faces I saw at the window!" said Amy.

"Who are you talking to?" asked Mum coming back into the room.

"The goblins," answered Amy. "Look!" She pointed to where the goblins had been, but they had dived behind a cushion when they heard Mum coming.

"I think you've been dreaming again," said Mum.

Amy lay on the sofa watching T.V., but after a while she felt hungry, and asked her mum for something to eat.

" You can't feel hungry after eating all that lunch," said Mum.

"But I didn't eat any lunch. The goblins did," whined Amy.

"Don't be silly. That was only a game."

"But they *did* eat it. They came downstairs from my doll's house," Amy explained.

"You've been having lots of funny dreams this morning while you've been poorly. There are no such things as goblins," laughed Mum.

"There are. They're real. I saw them. And they ate my lunch and now I'm hungry," said Amy.

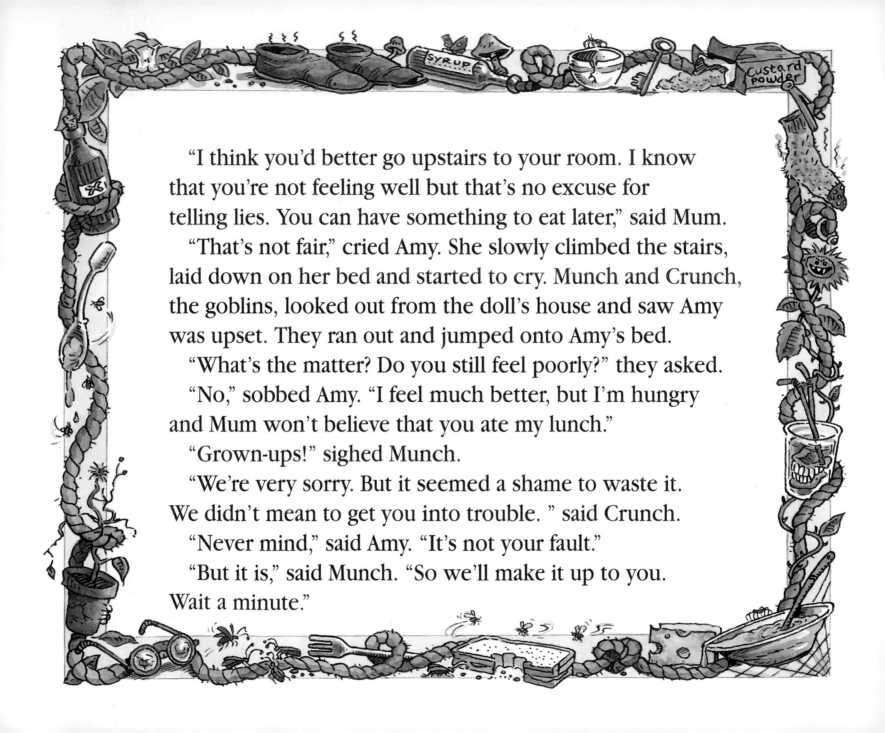

"I think you'd better go upstairs to your room. I know that you're not feeling well but that's no excuse for telling lies. You can have something to eat later," said Mum.

"That's not fair," cried Amy. She slowly climbed the stairs, laid down on her bed and started to cry. Munch and Crunch, the goblins, looked out from the doll's house and saw Amy was upset. They ran out and jumped onto Amy's bed.

"What's the matter? Do you still feel poorly?" they asked.

"No," sobbed Amy. "I feel much better, but I'm hungry and Mum won't believe that you ate my lunch."

"Grown-ups!" sighed Munch.

"We're very sorry. But it seemed a shame to waste it. We didn't mean to get you into trouble, " said Crunch.

"Never mind," said Amy. "It's not your fault."

"But it is," said Munch. "So we'll make it up to you. Wait a minute."

Munch whispered something to Crunch and they jumped down onto the floor and dashed into the doll's house. Amy sat and waited, but not for long. Soon Munch and Crunch came running out with trays filled with all the plastic food from the doll's house kitchen.

"I can't eat that," laughed Amy, "it's not real."

"Of course you can eat it," said Munch. "Watch."

With that Munch and Crunch held hands and started jumping up and down. As they did so they called out,

"Plastic food, you look so yummy. Become real, to fill my tummy."

With that there was a bright flash, and when Amy opened her eyes there in front of her was a real feast! "Oh, wow," she cried. "Thank you." Amy tucked into sandwiches, cakes, crisps, sausage rolls, biscuits and ice cream. After a while she said, "I'm full. I can't eat any more. Thank you." "We'd better clear up before your mum comes," said Crunch.

With another flash all the food vanished.

"We'd better go. Sorry you got into trouble, but I hope you enjoyed our lunch," said Crunch.

"Oh, I did. It was much nicer than a boiled egg," said Amy and they all laughed. They said goodbye and in a flash the goblins had gone.

Amy was just licking the last bit of ice cream from her lips when Mum came in with a tray of food.

"I thought that you might want some tea and biscuits," said Mum.

"Yes please," said Amy.

Mum sat on the bed and gave Amy the tray. Just then the phone rang and mum went to answer it. When she came back all the biscuits had gone.

"Who ate all those?" asked Mum.

"I did," replied Amy. "The goblins have gone home."